AS YOU WERE SAYING

AMERICAN WRITERS
RESPOND TO THEIR
FRENCH CONTEMPORARIES

Dalkey Archive Press
Champaign • London

Library of Congress Cataloging-in-Publication Data

As you were saying : American writers respond to their French
contemporaries / edited by Fabrice Rozié, Esther Allen, and Guy
Walter.
    p. cm.
  ISBN-13: 978-1-56478-474-2 (alk. paper)
  ISBN-10: 1-56478-474-6 (alk. paper)
  1. Short stories, French--Translations into English. 2. French
fiction--21st century--Translations into English. 3. Short stories,
American--21st century. I. Rozié, Fabrice. II. Allen, Esther.
III. Walter, Guy.
  PQ1278.A8 2007
  843′.0108092--dc22

                                                          2007004082

First Dalkey Archive edition, 2007
All rights reserved

Partially funded by the Illinois Arts Council, a state agency, the Cultural Services of the
French Embassy in the United States, the Villa Gillet, the Urban Community of Lyon,
and the University of Illinois, Urbana-Champaign.

Dalkey Archive Press is a nonprofit organization whose mission is to promote international
cultural understanding and provide a forum for dialogue for the literary arts.

www.dalkeyarchive.com

Printed on permanent/durable acid-free paper, bound in the United States of America, and
distributed throughout North America and Europe.

AS YOU WERE SAYING

CONTENTS

PREFACE

Not so long ago, American publishers viewed literature in translation as a prestigious addition to their catalogs. Today, the landscape has changed. Foreign fiction still has an air of the exotic and of being intellectually stimulating, but several factors have caused publishers to shy away from translations.

How do we reach new readers? How do we give French authors the opportunity to be read in translation in the U.S.? It seems that we must dream up something new—an inventive and generous idea. The volume that you hold in your hand was conceived as a literary game of which few examples exist—seven French writers wrote stories that were then sent to seven American writers, who either completed the original stories or wrote corresponding stories of their own.

Despite the relatively low number of translated titles published in the United States each year—the figure frequently referenced is that 3% of all books published are works in translation—in recent times there has been a more concentrated focus on finding new readers for these books. Major festivals that welcome thousands of visitors every year, such as PEN World Voices in New York, the L.A. Times Festival in Los Angeles, and the Miami Book Fair, were created in this spirit and have led to a substantial number of new readers of foreign authors. Collaborative programs such as Reading the World look to unite those people in America who get excited about encountering authors writing in French.

The exchange of translated texts between the French and American markets is currently quite unbalanced. As is the case in most countries, far more American works are translated abroad than works from other countries are translated into English. This is definitely the case in France where 40% of all available translations are of American texts and French authors have often read and been inspired by American literature. Unfortunately, American writers have far fewer chances to become acquainted with contemporary French authors, and to be influenced by their ideas and writings.

I hope you will enjoy this new dialogue between writers from two different worlds, so far apart and yet so similar. A special thank you to all of our American and French authors and to the seven American translators affiliated with the PEN American Center who graciously donated their time and knowledge in order to write and translate the short stories in this volume. The work in this volume blazes a trail for writers from France, helping them begin to make a name for themselves in this land across the ocean. All of these stories contribute to our common effort, co-funded by the Cultural Services of the French Embassy, the Villa Gillet in Lyon, and the Grand Lyon. Because I myself love books and was educated by reading literature from all over the world, I know that we all stand to unearth new parts of ourselves by discovering works in translation.

Jean-David Lévitte,
French Ambassador to the United States

TRANSLATLANTIC LIAISONS

The book you have in your hands is the latest episode in a romance that's been going on for centuries. The Marquis de Lafayette, Benjamin Franklin, Alexis de Tocqueville, Edgar Allan Poe, Charles Baudelaire, Henry James, Simone de Beauvoir, Nelson Algren, Marguerite Yourcenar, Julien Green, J.M.G. Le Clézio, Diane Johnson, and Paul Auster have all played their roles in it, as have many other writers from both sides of the Atlantic. All the accumulating years of reactions, analyses, theories, histories, descriptions, stories, passions, and translations collectively form a country of their own, somewhere between the United States and France, in that strange space where translations dwell, a bridge, a moveable feast, an entre-deux in which the writers of two cultures seek to know each other, shape each other, change each other, resist each other, merge with each other. Hard to think of another love affair between two nations as intense and longstanding as this particular translatlantic liaison.

Nevertheless, this book is entirely unique; nothing else quite like it has ever been done before. It emerged out of a long conversation between Guy Walter, director of the Villa Gillet in Lyon, Fabrice Rozié, the Literary Attaché at the French Cultural Services in New York, and Esther Allen of the PEN Translation Committee and the Center for Literary Translation at Columbia University. Under discussion was a prevailing perception that U.S. readers are currently indifferent to all writing in translation, French writing included—despite Flaubert, Balzac, Zola, Valéry, Sartre, Camus! Another widespread perception was also of concern: American novelists, so the story goes, influenced by television and film, adhere to a "strong narrative line" while their French counterparts muse on philosophical abstractions and purely internal dilemmas. How to see past this dichotomy?

Then the idea: why not have French and American novelists compose joint texts? The French novelists would compose the first part of each text, which would then be translated into English and given to the Americans, who would be free to respond to it in any way at all: continuation, variation, juxtaposition, contradiction, digression, closure—whatever reaction the initial text inspired. This was startling, audacious, and, on first contemplation, almost entirely unworkable. How on earth would we convince the novelists to agree to participate in such a stunt? Who would be brave enough, trusting enough, foolhardy enough, committed enough to the notion of the ongoing cultural engagement between France and the United States to risk it? Wasn't anti-Americanism nearly universal in France, especially among intellectuals, especially in recent years? Weren't all Americans confirmed francophobes, eating Freedom fries and Freedom toast and pouring the good Bordeaux down the drain as a patriotic duty to their President while gnashing their teeth over the terrible depredations wrought by French theory on the intellectual life of their nation?

But of course only a very strong passion could bring about such dramatic displays of mutual hostility. And therefore it's not so surprising that the reaction this project met with immediately was love. As you can see, a wide variety of extraordinary writers and translators instantly and enthusiastically engaged their time, talents, skills, energies, generosity and grace in this hazardous venture—and all for love. The only payment any of them has received is the leap of faith that made them willing to take a risk on the improbable possibility of an encounter, a dialogue, a connection—between two people, two languages, two cultures, two countries.

It's not up to us to analyze the results of this collective leap. But we do want you to know that the French writers whose work is included here all have other books available in English, so that language is no barrier to your further enjoyment of their work. And most of all we want to thank all the writers and translators who embarked on this adventure with us and thereby added a new chapter to the very old story of a love like no other.

Esther Allen

MARIE DARRIEUSSECQ

RICK MOODY

MARIE DARRIEUSSECQ

❖

The tracheotomy left him hoarse for a long time but in the end he got his normal voice back. And his shoulders were still the same. Sometimes when we were reading together in bed, I'd track the lines in his skin, which was thick and deeply creased, solidified like lava, with sags, notches, broken angles, flat patches dotted with melted pores, canyons and valleys, a relief map I knew by heart.

I would kiss his neck, the skinny Adam's apple, the damaged tendons, the little tracheotomy scar, but I stopped at the long scar that followed the jawline all the way around, as if his throat had been slit, disappearing into the hair on both sides.

Above it was the new face.

I got used to the burn very quickly; he was like that when we met. His face was rigid, "cardboard" he'd say, he couldn't make more than two or three generic expressions, but his voice, his gestures, all that went on inside his head—I don't know how I'd talk about that. You can describe a face, but it's hard to describe a person, all of a person, I mean.

I remember how we used to joke around, while we were waiting in line, for instance, when we got bored with the wait or someone was staring. All he had to do was go "Boo!" at just the right moment and the other person would start screaming. It was the first time I'd had so much fun with anyone.

When he was tired, he wore a scarf pulled up over his nose, and a hat. I called him the Invisible Man. His eyes he never hid. He had no eyelid left at all on the left. His eyeball formed perfect concentric circles: red, white, blue, and black. The right eye had lost its lashes, but when you saw him from that profile, with the scarf and hat, you couldn't tell a thing, just that the nose was a little short, maybe.

Occasionally, not very often, a stranger would speak to him. Sitting next to him on a bus, for example, or busy at a computer screen in an office. These strangers must either have been distracted or extremely myopic. When they looked at him full on, his face was like a fist smashing into theirs. But since they'd been the ones to speak first, they'd bravely try to go the distance. Their efforts quickly grew pathetic. They were too friendly, as if speaking to a mentally handicapped man or a little kid. They went on talking for too long, to show that nothing was bothering them, that they didn't see anything that could possibly bother them. And he'd let them dig themselves deeper and deeper, giving a big grin with his missing lips.

When he smoked, he'd clench the cigarette between his teeth and breathe noisily; it sounded like a straw sucking on an empty glass after you've finished the drink. People didn't dare ask him to put it out. They'd get hysterical when they smelled tobacco and realized someone was breaking the rules, but boy they screeched to a halt the instant they caught sight of his face.

The silence that would fall when we walked into a bar was something you had to hear. Men's faces, women's faces, all of them wondering what the hell I was doing with him. And going across borders with him, when the customs official looked at his passport, with a photo from before the burn—no one had ever dared ask him to have another one taken. Or when, with all the new security measures, he'd be asked to lower his scarf and take off his hat–the expression that would come across the official's face. The childish terror, the politically correct reflexes, disgust warring with charity, the absolute fear of the other, all of it nakedly clear.

But his sacrosanct exhaustion was gaining the upper hand. To think that this is the same man who protested when I wanted to have a tummy tuck, *your stomach's fine just the way it is,* always the same old song, but the moment the experimental protocol was launched he was off and running. And he went about it so well, charming the surgeons, the shrinks, the whole team, that he was chosen for the first complete face transplant.

The donor's family, his wife in particular, had also taken several tests and signed a pledge never to try to find us. All we knew was that the donor was more or less the same age, had more or less the same skin color, and had died suddenly in a distant country.

I could never bring myself to look him in the face. Above the half-circle of the scar, the skin was quite smooth, ruddy, with a heavy beard. When I looked for his profile, his strange right profile, I'd see a long nose with cheeks stuck on either side, still a little stiff, like the latex masks thieves wear in movies. The eyebrows and forehead were supple, almost too supple, like flowing water or wax, as if the face were

5

about to come off. I didn't dare touch it. Every morning he shaved like a teenager, with great concentration and effort. He shaved off the beard that was not his. Apparently, hair follicles survive for several hours after death, and I'm telling you, it was a heavy beard. With the razor, he'd shave stripes in the shaving cream across that face. That was the only way I could look at him: in the mirror, from behind his back, watching the shaving cream disappear.

The face was neither ugly nor handsome, I don't know. It was a stranger's face, a face that could have belonged to anyone. There was still a weird rigidity, the movement wasn't quite right yet, but he never missed a physical therapy session and we were assured that in time the face would move in a natural way, quite normally.

Even his gaze had changed, because, as I've come to realize, eyelids are what make a gaze. An eyeball has no gaze, no expression. Intensity, yes, I remember the intensity, the unblinking rage, the wicked laugh. But then, with eyelids, he just looked like a nice person.

Translated by Esther Allen

RICK MOODY

❖

One day I woke to find that she was no longer attractive to me. Spring, a time of horticultural vainglory. There was a nice breeze blowing in, there was some sunshine. Her gentlest smile greeted me upon waking. I rolled away and faced the wall.

We had a lot in common. The same black sense of humor Nothing disappointed me more than sentimentality. We mustered a small, mobile tactical unit for the purposes of wiping it out. We used to go on bus trips in search of children to startle or terrify. On one such occasion, I scanned the aisles for a rosy-cheeked victim and, locating him, with a suitable flourish I twisted my face into a mask of woe and anguish: "I too was once young!" The boy shrank away in horror, blubbering like a girl. What a good laugh we had!

Why she picked me out of the crowd in the first place, only her psychiatrists can say. Still, she wasn't alone. There were women who wanted what a man like myself brought with him: recovery rooms, bouts of insomnia, white rages, liquid diets. Most of these women left in tears.

I saw her first. At a dinner party. I was wearing a hooded sweat-shirt and a scarf, as I did among friends and strangers alike. In truth, I wore the outfit so that I could stare, a pastime largely denied me. She was on the short side, svelte, with dirty blond hair that she wore to her shoulders. She had the posture of a dancer, perhaps one often injured. Her lips were a routine crimson. She didn't smoke, she never ate as far as I could tell, and she drank like a soldier. We often polished off a couple of bottles of wine with lunch and then kept right on with our spree until, at night, we tumbled into unconsciousness.

It was when intoxicated that she wanted me. She didn't want me in a delicate, refined way; she lusted like a stray cat. Everything depended on brutality. She would strip off my clothes, heedless of their fastenings. She would sink finger-nails into me, there were often bite marks. She drew blood. How to explain my gratitude?

When, after some years, she embarked on the first of her own "revisions," as she called them, I was surprised enough to misunderstand the impulse. A gray hair or two had been harvested. She had a disagreeable scar dating to an immemo-rial mishap in a childhood attic. She didn't scar well, she had the audacity to say, and wanted to improve on what nature had wrought. Not long after, I came home to find her on the sofa, lips pursed. "They're going to straighten my nose."

Then she began composing her elaborate fabrications. Ordinarily, in my romantic past, the women came to their senses. The isolation toughened them up. They stumbled invigorated out of the flames of my disconsolation. After they'd snuck around for a while, they confessed, wept, and packed.

Not this time. As I became more and more erratic, as I fell into an inertia wherein I did little but collect my disability payments, she seemed to grow ever more exotic. She was luminous, increasingly beautiful, like some poisonous toadstool. With every fingertip I laid upon her, she seemed to grow more stridently perfect. She was a work of art, and I was the wage-earning desperado in the empty gallery.

I could catalogue the procedures for you, because I made it my business to do so. I could list kilos of flesh, bits of bone and sinew that had been trimmed from her and packed into those refreshing little medical waste baggies, to be incinerated in a featureless out-building. She lied about the procedures and she devoted herself to ever more Byzantine deceits. Her features came to resemble a large cat of some African genus, a sleek, remorseless panther. Or she was a raptor hovering in the updrafts. Evidently the surgeons kept near the pictures of these animals as they sliced away some more of her and readied the implants.

In May, we intended to go to a masquerade. The hosts were friends of hers, of course. I had long since run through my own supply of friends. She'd encountered this pair—she was so excited to tell me—while looking for a *job*. Of course, I was adamant that she avoid work, because my condition was delicate and I needed constant attention. I had enough money to keep us underfed. And yet behind my back she'd arranged a job interview. And I would *never guess* who she met while there!

I ascertained that she had also "improved" on her breasts. Her breasts seemed even more adorable and muscular than they had been when I first gazed upon them. They were like little Victorian pincushions. She must have undergone the procedure while I was traveling home on the occasion of my father's death. It was the longest we'd been apart.

When I returned, I began following her on her daily peregrinations—when I could do so from a discreet distance. I believed, for example, that she planned a sexual liaison with the couple throwing the masquerade. There were suitors behind every streetlamp.

For the big party, she intended to get me up as a prince. She spent a week or so scouring the fabric shops of the neighborhood for dusty bolts of simulated finery. Meanwhile, I was to make a selection for her, but the only costume I could think of was the Angel of Death.

So: I woke the morning of the masquerade ball with the bleak but refreshing impression that I no longer desired her. I didn't care for the years when she had made life tolerable, I didn't care for her pert, flawless breasts. I didn't care for the muffled candlelight of our devotion. Indeed, it was her generosity that squeezed the breath out of me.

It was then that I hit on the idea for the surgery. A diabolical stratagem, true enough, and therefore perfect. There was no difficulty with the doctors and psychiatrists. There wasn't a suffering wretch in all of Europe who looked quite as bad as I did. I had only to attempt a smile to bring good men to tears. The panel of experts concurred. No doubt it was only a matter of time before some lad, silly and reckless, finished making use of his own face.

In the end, you see, she was only interested in me for my looks.

CAMILLE LAURENS

ROBERT OLEN BUTLER

CAMILLE LAURENS AND
ROBERT OLEN BUTLER

"SHE HAD WAITED FOR THIS"

❖

She had waited for the day to dawn and the sun to set, for the pigeons to coo and the night to crawl by, for her father to return, to appear around the curve of the woods, his face against the windowpane, his lips creating a white mist on the glass inside of which he'd draw a heart, for her mother to say something, for someone to explain things to her, for the bell to ring, for the vacation to begin, for Sundays to end, for the coach to arrive and her fairy godmother to come, for the prince to set her free, for her breasts to grow, her period to start, for God to manifest Himself, for Thy kingdom to come. She waited for the phone to ring, hundreds of times, in a corner crumpled in a heap on the floor, balled up on her bed, pierced by the silence to the point of hallucination, in the end confusing *I languish* and *I listen*—please hold on, I'm here—she'd waited a hundred years. She waited for the polish to dry, the mask to set, the cream to work, for the water to boil, the dough to rise, the cake to bake; she waited for the mailman to pass, hundreds of times, sitting on the first step, hoping for mail, the anticipated letter, the beloved handwriting; she'd waited to be seen, to be noticed, to be addressed, to be invited, to be kissed, to be apparent, to be called, to be recognized—we are doing our utmost to shorten your wait.

She had waited for boys, for men, on station platforms, in airports, waiting rooms of vanished footsteps, the train, bus, plane, taxi, the ambulance, paramedics, help, she'd waited for help. She'd waited at the doctor's, the dentist's, the grocer's, the movies, the ticket window and the cash register, she waited her turn—to be given a ticket, to be assigned a role, a place, to be shown a seat, a row, to have an illness and a remedy revealed, to be given an order, a function, a solution, to be given meaning; she'd waited for her time, the right time, the perfect time, she'd waited for happiness.

She'd waited for her period, the test tube result came quickly, she expected a child. She'd waited for the event, the happy event, she'd waited for life, for D-day, the delivery, she'd waited nine months.

She'd waited for the first cry, the first word, the first smile, the first tooth, the first step. She'd waited for the test results, the surgeon's opinion, his look, his words, his explanation—don't expect a miracle. She'd waited for him to wake up, to open his eyes, waited for God to save him, may His will be done, she waited for him to be resurrected.

She'd waited for oblivion, for mourning to end, for grief to ease, for the heart to close down. She'd waited for a word of consolation, an expression of solace, waited for him to understand, be patient, accept, waited for him to wait—don't leave me, I am yours. She'd waited for him to speak to her, explain to her, answer her: what was the matter? What had she done? What would become of them? What's wrong, wait, what have I done to you? She'd waited for him to come back, to say "I love you," for him to love her, to tell her so, she'd waited for a loving word, the lyrics of the song *I'll wait for you day and night, I'll wait for your return, always*. She'd waited for it to come back, to begin again, to have it work, prevail, change, end. She'd waited for it to pass, subside, diminish, fade.

She'd waited for it to disappear.

She'd waited for springtime, summer, for it to be fine, for the rain to stop, to cease. She'd waited for the pharmacy to open, the bar to close, the party to start, her head to explode. She'd waited a long time, everywhere, for the lovely tango of intoxication and the toboggan of sleep, the spinning top of gin and the rocketing highs—make sure you have left everything on board.

She had forgotten her father, his age when he left, the house, the address, the neighbors, the teacher, the school. She'd forgotten his eyes, his nose, his mouth, his voice, his scent, his laughter. She'd forgotten the dance steps she'd learned, the basics of the guitar, the recipe for French toast, the price of a baguette in those years. She'd forgotten when, where, how—the accusations, arguments, blows, the anguish, the tears—she had forgotten why. She'd forgotten everything that happened in the beginning, absolutely everything: the breast, the baby bottle, the crying, the tickling, the thumb, the buntings, the diapers, the dark, the night, the loneliness, the caresses, the voice, the toys, games, stuffed animals, the carriage, the stroller, the colors, the smells—she'd forgotten the early childhood, the down time, the cadence. She'd forgotten to wind her watch, buy bread, take out the trash, look at photos, call, smile, meet her appointments, say thank you, yes, no, excuse me, to ask why. She'd forgotten to attend her mother's funeral—but what are you waiting for, poor girl? She'd forgotten names, dates, schedules, faces, dreams, she'd forgotten other people. Forgotten that you could be happy or unhappy, that it depended, forgotten what it depended on. She'd forgotten laws, orders, deadlines, instructions, she'd forgotten rights, duties, rules. She'd fallen into memory's hole, sunk into oblivion.

She'd forgotten when she made the decision. She merely waited for her time and her time had come—the right time.

She sat down in the waiting room. *The drama occurred around 7:30 PM in the*—it was last night's newspaper, someone must have left it there on the little table. The seats were a washed-out yellow, the wallpaper a shabby blue. Don't forget to, said the peeled-off poster on the wall. The crossword had been started:

3 Down. Shortens as it lies down.
4 Across. They all wound, the last one kills.

She waited for the door to open as she filled in the squares, a matter of killing time.

Her hand moved down and across, across and down, building words one square at a time until she realized that the hand had stopped. It was poised above the paper and she found herself staring at the grid of words. She knew this was one of those moments when, waiting in the faint hiss made by the creeping seconds of her life, she was apt to forget. The hand, holding the ballpoint pen, began to tremble. *I am . . .* she said to herself, intending to fill in the purpose of her visit to this place. No words came to finish the sentence. *I am . . .* she began again, intending at least to fill in her name. Again, she could think of nothing.

She thought to step through the outer door, to see if there was a sign that would tell her. But before she could, the door to the office opened. Framed there, backlit by the bright morning light pouring through a window inside, was the silhouette of a man. Small, somewhat stooped, his face in shadow, wearing a snap-brim hat.

"Come in," he said. He turned.

She put aside the newspaper, the pen. She rose, she followed, passing through the door and into the brightness of the office. The man circled the desk and sat down in a wooden swivel chair, which squealed from its swivel joint as if it were in terrible pain.

She still could not remember why she was here. But she'd become adept at following the flow of a life she did not fully recognize.

She sat in a chair before the desk and waited for the man to speak.

The top of his desk was empty except for an unlit gooseneck lamp and a cordless phone. He placed his hands face down before him. He gazed at her. Rather, she assumed he was gazing at her, for she could not clearly see his face. The bright light from the window behind him made his face a dark, undifferentiated shadow.

At last he said, "Madame Laurens." She recognized this as her married name.

She nodded. He waited. She waited. She sensed he wanted her to speak, perhaps to state her business. She laid one of her hands over the other in her lap. She focused on her shallow breath. In and out. In and out. She would wait.

"You left the message on my machine," he said.

This did not seem familiar. She did not speak.

"It was not clear," he said.

"Not clear," she said.

He waited. She waited. Then she said, "Can you play it?"

He did not respond.

"The message," she said.

He did not stir. She listened to her own breath for a few more moments, and then one of his lands lifted up and moved to the phone base. He pushed a button and she could hear a woman's voice. She inferred that it was her own.

"Monsieur," the voice said. "I am . . ." And here the voice hesitated for one second and then another, and just before the machine automatically ended the message, it said, ". . . Madame Laurens. I must see you at once. I am in need of you. I will come to your office first thing tomorrow morning and I will wait."

The phone clicked and the message ended. The man's hand returned to the desktop.

"You see?" he said.

"Yes."

"My services . . ." he began and then broke off with a weary lift and turn of one hand. "I can open a file. You must say what you need."

"Yes," she said.

But she did not say. She and the man in the swivel chair sat in silence and they both waited. She could feel his gaze coming out of the shadow that was his face.

Then at last he sighed and he leaned back. He swiveled to his right in the chair, his invisible gaze leaving her. This time the cry of the chair was faint. "Those who come to me are in distress," he said.

"Yes."

"When it is . . . domestic . . . they often don't even understand what it is that they need."

She nodded, though he was not looking at her now.

He said, "They want to find something. Or lose something."

"They wait, they forget," she said.

"Yes," he said, and then he fell silent.

She tried to remember why she'd called this man. She tried to remember what it was that she needed, other than to remember, though she was not sure she needed even that. Perhaps she had waited all this time so that she would not have to remember. Yes. This was a lesson she had learned and it was hard to forget: If she could not remember what she needed, then she did not need anything. She lifted her hands and pressed at her temples.

And for a moment she forgot everything. Everything. In her head was only this: the buzz of the silence of the room, a distant car horn, the slip of her own breath, a faint creak of the man's chair.

"Tell me," he said.

"I heard a car horn in the distance," she said.

His head turned back toward her. The gaze returned from the shadow.

"I placed one hand over the other in my lap," she said. Silence between them.

"Why are you here?" he said.

"Why?"

"Yes."

"This body I'm in," she said. "There is life in it. I still breathe. I move here and there."

"But that's true of everyone outside this window," he said. "And yet it is you sitting before me."

"What do you do for others?" she said.

"Others?"

"What is the thing you most often do?"

He turned back to her in his chair. She waited. She'd asked a question that perhaps would shed some light on why she was here. *Madame Laurens*, she whispered to herself so she would not forget.

"I look for the hidden things," said the man before her in the snap-brim hat sitting in the wooden swivel chair framed in the bright window. "The lost things."

"That's your job," she said.

"Yes."

"To look."

"Yes."

And she remembered a little thing. *I can look*, the man had said. Another man. Another office. In another city.

"But you must tell me what you are looking for," said the man before her now.

And she remembered another thing. In the other city. He had said, *He changed his name to Laurent Mézières.*

"It was an irony," she said.

"An irony?"

"That you are also a detective," she said.

And she rose and she circled his desk and he swiveled to face her and he leaned back in his chair, perhaps a little afraid, not knowing what she was doing, and she put her two hands on the arms of the chair and turned it even further and he did not resist. She put her hand under his chin and lifted his face to the light, and she remembered a nose narrow and straight and flared at the nostrils. She remembered eyes the color of wet concrete. She remembered a wide mouth with thin lips as if pressed always together in agitation. She remembered a coffee-colored mole at the outside edge of the right eyebrow. This face in the light.

"I am your daughter," she said.

Translated by Marjolijn de Jager

JACQUES ROUBAUD

RAYMOND FEDERMAN

JACQUES ROUBAUD

THE JOSEPHUS PROBLEM

❖

The battle had drawn to a close. For the defenders, the battle was lost. The battle had been won by the assailants. After fifty-three days of siege, the fortress Jotapata, which had been built by Joshua in Galilee to the north of Sepphoris, had fallen at the hands of the Romans because of a deserter's betrayal. Thirty-five thousand perished. More than eleven thousand—men, women, children—would be sold as slaves. In the subterranean room where the last survivors—among them, the leader of the insurrection, Eleazar ben Simon of Saab—had taken refuge before the legions' final assault, Vespasian's soldiers found the corpses of forty blindfolded men on the ground. They had all died in the same way: from a sword's blow to the back of the head, at the root of the neck. Forty dead. Forty dead and one survivor. Who declared his name to be Josephus.* In his left hand he held his sword, drenched in blood.

"Who are you?" asked Vespasian when the prisoner was brought before him in chains. "How is it that you are still alive, when all your comrades are dead?" Wounded during the fighting, the commander of the Roman armies was lying on a litter, his son Titus standing at his side. "Father," said Titus, "what do we care about this rebel's tales? Send him to Nero!" Vespasian silenced his son and repeated the question.

And Josephus responded: "We had decided not to let ourselves be captured alive only to be slaughtered or sold as slaves to Rome. Yet none of us wanted to die a shameful death by our own hand. Some of us wanted to attempt one last attack against the Romans, but nothing guaranteed that we would all be killed in the course of this final battle. The soldiers, with information from the traitor, must have received the order to find and capture us. Time was of the essence. The sound of the slaughter was drawing near. Soon our hideout would be discovered, and it would be too late. Our leader, when he was convinced our fight was lost, thought long and hard about how to reach the goal each and every one of us desired: to die, but not by Roman hands, and not by unforgivable suicide. So he proposed the following:

"Let us arrange ourselves in a circle. Let us then sit, blindfolded, swords in hand, heads bowed, our bare necks exposed. When I give the signal, he whom by fate's choice is first to act will lift the blindfold that prevented him from seeing, rise, and send his neighbor to his anticipated death. He will then resume his position and await the blow he will receive in his turn. Gradually, with no changing of places, the dead will replace the living one by one. In this way, forty of us will escape both slavery and suicide. The circle's last survivor, should he not depart this life while fighting, will be the sole sufferer of either of these two disgraces. He will have sacrificed himself for the honor of us all."

Vespasian and Titus listened attentively to the rebel who stood calm and fearless before them. Josephus paused, and then began anew: "Having spoken, our leader drew a circle on the cave's floor, set the youngest among us in the first position, then placed himself where he had decided to be, and bid us to position ourselves where we desired. When I saw where he had placed himself, thinking about how our

24

sacrifice would unfold, I understood that he had chosen to be the last survivor. I understood this. I went to sit at his side, took the same posture as my comrades, and placed the blindfold over my eyes, my sword close at hand."

"And yet you are here, and all the others are dead. How do you explain this?"

"He Who Decides All Things wanted it so," responded Josephus. "And do you know why? So that I, Josephus, might be able to address you, Vespasian, and your son Titus, in order to make the following prophecy. Listen, then, to what I have to say:

I PREDICT THAT YOU WILL BE EMPEROR
AND THAT AFTER YOU, YOUR SON TITUS
WILL BE EMPEROR AS WELL.

"Rebel," said Vespasian, "my gods do not acknowledge your God, and I therefore have no faith in your prediction. I know full well why you flatter me by offering me, by offering us this image of a future of shared imperial glory. You want to escape the slavery that awaits you. But just as I consider worthless an oracle made in the name of a divinity whose existence I deny, I likewise do not believe it is some supernatural intervention that has allowed you to be the sole survivor of the bloody ceremony you described. Pray clarify this matter for us."

"With pleasure," said Josephus. "I was faced with an apparently unsolvable problem. According to the rule decreed by our leader, my chances of survival were very precisely nil...............................**"

Josephus explained everything, and his account appeared so ingenious to Vespasian that the Roman leader immediately freed him from his chains, made him his advisor, and brought him back to Rome with him for the Triumph.

He thought that there was a chance his own gods would decide to follow the advice of such a clever man, if only to reward his cleverness. And Vespasian did indeed become emperor, succeeding Vitellius, and his son Titus too became ruler of the Empire in his turn . . .

---

*Or "Josippus," if one goes by the Slavonic version of Josephus's chronicle. The Latin account of the events, called the *Josephus Latinus*, is wrongly attributed to Hegesippus, an author from the second century AD. It was no doubt penned by Ambrosius, Bishop of Milan in the fourth century. "Hegesippus" is in all probability a corruption of "Josephus."

**A lacuna in the text of the Chronicle has caused Josephus's explanation to disappear, but the reader can easily reconstruct the method he used to survive.

Translated by the students of Fr185A, Literary Translation (Fall 2006), Yale University, in alphabetical order: Lulu Cheng, Heather Freeman, Yonah Freemark, William Griffin, Emily Gruen, Carmen Lee, Suchitra Paul, Tiffany Pham, Daniel Schlosberg, Kathryn Takabvirwa, Jake Velker, Meredith Williams, and Mei-Lun Xue, with their professor, Alyson Waters

RAYMOND FEDERMAN

Yesterday I bought a new tape recorder—and today I recorded a story on my new recorder—this is the story—I call it—

THE CARCASSES

❖

I am sitting in my study—that's how the story I recorded begins—I am sitting in my study—in San Diego California— close to the sun—where I moved four years ago to be with myself and finish my work—I am sitting in my study looking out of the window at the splendid view before me—incredible—the valley the mountains the trees the sky the birds— beautiful—I'm having a good day—I feel great—I am working on *My Body in Nine Parts*—the English version—I am working on my nose today—I take a break to smoke a joint and look up at the view before me—incredible—a thought comes to me—when you die all this gets extinguished—nothing more to see—it's like plunging into a big black hole—everything becomes dark—but then it occurs to me that to think that—to plunge into the darkness implies the possibility of an after . . .—another life in the darkness—the possibility of some kind of existence after you disappear into that blackness— could I have been wrong all my life—no—no—I'm not going to fall for that meta-pata-physical crap—no magic trick—no divine intervention—I am human—I am conscious of being human and mortal—but let's assume for a moment that you are dead—and there is the possibility of an after-life in the darkness—so here you are among all the dead carcasses in the zone of carcasses—yes that's what this story is about—the carcasses—here they are—the old ones that have been here for a long time—and the new ones that have just arrived—all piled on top of one another waiting for their turn to be transmuted—to be given another life—transmutation does not happen all at once—does not happen instantly the moment you become a carcass—carcasses are not reincarnated the moment they become carcasses—there is a waiting period—a kind of incubation—if I dare say—so here you are waiting your turn—no magic trick as I said—just that you have to wait for the authorities to decide—yes let's call them that— the authorities—only the authorities have the power to decide when it's your turn to be transmuted—they call you— hey you over there come here—you scramble your way out of the pile of carcasses and report to the authorities and they tell you we're sending you back—doesn't have to be on the planet Earth—carcasses come from all sorts of places in the universe— the place where the carcasses are piled up is a separate zone in the great void of the universe—nobody knows where it is—it's like a huge department store—like Walmart—and there carcasses of all sizes of all types all shapes all forms all colors—all of them formless—wait to be transmuted—carcasses cannot demand of the authorities under what form they want to be sent back—they have no voice—they have to accept the authorities' decision—so your turn comes and you are told that you are going back as an insect—yes—as a fly—imagine yourself now living the life of a fly—ok it's a short life—*une vie éphémère*—but still—what is your main purpose in life—your *raison d'être*—to buzz around—to bug the shit out of the other species—buzz around the eyes of cows who try to smack you with their tails—buzz around humans—shit on their window panes or TV screens—still it's a life—but one day you land on the arm or the top of the head of a human and—bang—he slaps you with his hand—crushes you—splashes you—and you're dead—what kind of a life was that—so here you are back among the carcasses—oh you're back already the others say to you—I mean those carcasses who are still waiting to be transmuted—and again you wait your turn—well this time your turn comes quick—no reason given—you come back as a flower—a lovely red rose in the suburban garden of some *nouveau riche* on the coast of California—and you're proud because you know you're beautiful and you smell good—the ladies who come to play bridge look at you and say—oh what a beautiful rose—but then one day the lady of the house tells the maid to get flowers in the garden and put them on the dining room table—so here comes the maid with her clippers and she cuts you off and sticks you in a vase full of water—and soon the water starts smelling foul and it's unbearable—and you begin to wither—and the lady of the house says to the maid get rid of that dead flower—and the maid throws you into the garbage and empties the smelly water into the toilet—but still it was a life—and now you are back among the carcasses—what kind of life was that—and now you wait again—this time a very long time—maybe a couple of centuries—even more—but you don't know how long because time does not exist in the carcass zone—or rather carcasses have no sense of time—finally the authorities call you and tell you that you are needed among the lions of Africa—there is a shortage of virile male lions on planet Earth—and so they are sending you back to be a lion in Kenya with three sexy lionesses and a bunch of cubs—and it's a good life—every fifteen minutes—this has been carefully observed by expert lion observers—every fifteen minutes one of the lionesses comes over licks you and begs for a little humping—so you rise from your dreamy slumber in the shade of a tree—hump the lioness and go back to the shadow of the tree where you continue dreaming what a good life this is—plenty to eat—the lionesses

see to that—lots of gazelle meat—and it's fun to hump the
lionesses and play with the little cubs—but one day a bunch
of humans of different colors come to hunt you—the black
ones are half naked and dance around—the white ones wear
funny colonial hats and have rifles and they drink a lot—but
they are not here to make a carcass out of you—they want you
alive—they want to capture you—and they do with a big
net—then they stick you in a box and ship you to what they
call the civilized world—lucky for you—they don't put you
in the Buffalo zoo where you would have to spend the rest of
your temporary earthly life in a cage wallowing in your own
shit—freezing your balls in the snows of Buffalo—and with
no sexy lioness to hump because now—for lack of exercise in
the wilderness—you're incapable of getting it up—but lucky
for you—they put you in the San Diego zoo—and build for
you what they call a natural environment—of course it's
fake—this is California—there is nothing natural about this
environment they build for you—it's pure Hollywood
decor—you know that—you know it's fake—but you pretend
it's really nice—and to make the humans feel good and happy
so they don't send you to the Buffalo zoo once in a while you
roar and show your teeth—but you're bored in this phony
Walt Disney environment—most of the time you sleep—or
pretend to be asleep—especially when they bring their little
kids to look at you in fear—they would like you to look and
act ferocious—so once in a while a human pokes you in the
ass so you can roar—what kind of a life is that—okay they
bring you these big chunks of meat—lots of beef—but one
day one of the pieces of meat they give you comes from a sick
cow and you die—you die of the mad cow disease—still it
was a life—and you're back among the carcasses—well I
won't go into all the possible animal or human or vegetable
forms you could come back as—but imagine yourself as a

radish—what kind of a life that would be—or an artichoke—
okay a tree—a big majestic tree—that would be okay for a
while—but then all the other trees around become jealous
because you're taller—or because your trunk is bigger than
theirs—or your leaves greener—but still it's a life—then one
day some humans come with a big saw and cut you down to
pieces and burn you—what kind of a life was that—and here
you are back in the zone of carcasses—and while waiting for
your turn to come again you think—well I know carcasses are
not supposed to be able to think—but for the commodity of
this story let's just say that they are capable of a certain mental
cogitation—so you cogitate—why can't I have a voice in the
decision of what I want to become next—why can't I make up
my own . . .—well I was going to say mind—let's just say my
own carcassness—on this matter—and since you were once a
writer in a previous transmutation—and have not forgotten
the art of writing you compose a very stylish message
addressed to the authorities asking if maybe the carcasses
couldn't have a say in the process of their transmutation—this
stirs up things in the carcass zone—there are discussions—
debates—polls—demonstrations—and all sorts of things like
that—and finally the authorities agree—the carcasses can
have a say in what they want to be when transmuted—so
now the carcasses have a chance to come in front of the
authorities to discuss what they would like to become—it's a
very complex and lengthy process but eventually you decide
for yourself what you want to become—for instance me I
often said that if I were to come back I would want to come
back as a gladiator so that I could lead a revolt against the
Roman emperor—or come back as a musketeer—like the
Duke of Nevers who invented *la botte de Nevers*—or as a
Italian lover—like Casanova—or as—as—as—damn it's not easy
to decide for oneself what one wants to come back as—so many

possibilities—good ones—bad ones—unbearable ones—dumb ones—some so short it doesn't even pay to be transmuted—this is why I think the best thing to do here—I mean here in this story—is to let readers decide themselves what they would like to come back as when they become carcasses—and when this story is published—I will insist that the last page of the story be blank so that readers can write what they want to become in their next life and in so doing contribute to this story—of course someday in the near future—the way science is making progress—carcasses may be able to come back as objects—it may not be a great life—but still a life—imagine coming back as a stove or an electric razor—or a toilet seat—just thinking about that horrifies me—or better yet—as a golf club—that would be an interesting life—here you are a brand new Taylor Made Titanium 360 driver with a graphite shaft—not a bad life—well at least until the golfer decides that you're driving him crazy with the way you slice the ball and buys another carcass reincarnated as a King Cobra 560 driver with an anti-slice shaft—and throws you in the garbage—imagine what a life that would be—still a life—by the time I finished recording this story it was dark outside my window and the splendid view had vanished into the night—

LYDIE SALVAYRE

RIKKI DUCORNET

LYDIE SALVAYRE

IN PRAISE OF UGLINESS

Adapted from a French tale, Charles Perrault's
"Riquet à la houppe."

❖

Riquet is ugly. Which has its advantages. Women, for example, do not importune him with their repellent romantic requests. Riquet can thus devote himself entirely to his work: managing stock options for the XXL company.

❖

Riquet has a cowlick. And his mother (a real bitch) called him Cowlick Ricky.

Unhappy Riquet has tried flattening his hair with extreme gel, extra-hold hairspray, and nutrient-rich pomade; nothing works. No sooner anaesthetized by the various ointments, his cowlick straightens, rears up, and asserts itself, arrogant.

Because, you see, Riquet's cowlick is in constant insurrection. And strong-arm tactics work no better than more democratic approaches. Whether Riquet cajoles or mistreats it, the failure is the same. (And we should note that excessive fussing over of a cowlick, child, cock, or any other excrescent body is considered, by the wary, as a proven form of abuse.)

His cowlick is his sorrow. The thorn in his side.

His cowlick is a sorrow that nothing can cure. An extremely unworthy sorrow, moreover, because while ordinary ugliness can sometimes take on a certain panache, the unsightliness of a forelock in disorder is always frankly ridiculous.

All Riquet can do to counter the mockery of others is to make fun of himself. Which he does very often. And not without masochism. His shrink says so.

❖

Fortunately, Riquet is rich. Which compensates for his unattractiveness very effectively.

If he's seized by the desire to go yachting—bam!—he calls his bank and an hour later he's on a yacht, purchased from Mangul, emir of Beleganzo.

The same goes for women: He opens his wallet, they open his fly, all in the same motion. It works every time.

❖

His enormous fortune opens doors for him everywhere: parties at Castel, charity galas (very fashionable), inaugurations, commemorations, parades, gallery openings, orgies, and other extremely eminent cultural events.

At a party hosted by Sharon Stone (I.Q. 136), his best friend, an unpleasant and disheveled person, introduces him to her sister, who is beautiful and sad. As soon as he sees this woman, Riquet falls precipitously in love. Because not only is his friend's sister as beautiful as she is sad, she is also very stupid. Which, of course, only adds to her glamour.

And besides, she gives blowjobs. They say.

❖

Riquet thinks of his friend's sister often.

I'm in love, he says to himself. What a disaster!

Though objectively he feels he has no chance of

catching her eye, nonetheless he decides one fine evening to confess his ardor.

That day, he spends at least an hour trying to flatten the obstinate cowlick.

In vain.

Would scalp implants help? Perhaps such an embellishment would provide competition, canceling out, through pure interplay, the solitary and dominating tuft? It's a question Riquet asks himself very seriously before going to face his destiny. Either that, or he thinks: I could cut my hair like Brad Pitt's, or shave my head—that's fashionable. . . .

Before the appointment, he rolls a joint to give him courage and forget about his defect, which he calls his "thing."

The young lady, whom he thinks of often while jerking off, is waiting for him in a coffee shop. Riquet sits down beside her and after touching his cowlick (this gesture is an obsession, what can I say, it's a tic, it's a toc, it's a disease) declares himself as follows:

I cannot understand how a person as beautiful as you can be as sad as you appear to be, for though I have been fortunate enough to know an infinite number of beautiful women, I assure you I have never seen anyone whose beauty approaches yours.

The girl is impressed by the elegant speech, accustomed as she is to the rude laconism of her other suitors whose vocabularies are limited to about two hundred words. But the poor girl can only utter a truism in response. So you say, she says. The trite expression barely out of her mouth, she becomes self-conscious and ashamed.

Riquet does not hold her truism against her. Quite the contrary. Truisms, he assures her, have a tranquilizing effect on his mind, which is constantly fevered, boundless and infinite. Moreover, he plans to write a small opus soon on the beneficial effect of truisms on the soul and the role they play in sexual happiness.

Beauty, he goes on, while touching his cowlick (because Riquet is moved, and when he is moved, his compulsive gesture only gets worse), is such an advantage that ... To put it simply, my dear, your beauty distracts me, I've got you under my skin, and I'd like very much for us to sleep together.

And I, the young girl replies, would rather be as ugly as you and have your mind than be as beautiful and idiotic as I am.

Riquet, whose chivalrous heart (because the ugly ones often have a chivalrous heart) is just waiting for the chance to show itself, flies to the aid of this maiden who so cruelly rebukes herself. Nothing, he assures her, better proves that one has a first-rate mind than believing one does not! In fact, the more intelligence you have, the more you think you lack. And the more you think you know, the more you know that you don't know.

I don't understand all your talk, the young girl exclaims, overwhelmed with sadness, and I have a headache. Do you have an aspirin? I know I'm a complete idiot, and that destroys me.

❖

Riquet goes back home rather discouraged, his cowlick in disarray, like his heart.

But the following day, he's back in fine form. (The ugly ones, armored as they are against the pangs of appearance, have a resilience—see Sartre!—that the beautiful ones, preoccupied with their plumage and pettiness, do not.) From here on out, Riquet decides, he will devote himself to devising arguments to convince this beautiful girl that true stupidity is not what she thinks it is at all.

With this secret intention, he invites her to dine with—guess who?—Joel Laplon, one of France's most popular and self-centered writers (these things go hand-in-hand), who sputters and pontificates and spews a few factoids and then leaves, extremely pleased with himself. That, Riquet says to her later, is a person afflicted with true stupidity, a stupidity acquired at great expense and more effort than you can imagine. I regret to inform *you*, young lady—he adds in a mischievous tone—that you cannot hold a candle to that man's stupidity. Alas, you must bow before this pompous ass!

❖

The story ends as in a sitcom (isn't that a shame for literature?). Riquet drinks in the words of the beautiful girl, whom love has magically imbued with intelligence. Her fingers caress his cowlick tenderly, and then his crotch. What happened? A supernatural act? A charm? A miracle from heaven? Children will understand without having it explained to them. The rest can go to hell.

Translated by Jeanine Herman

RIKKI DUCORNET

LA GOULUE IN RETIREMENT

❖

Once La Goulue got old and fat, *ces messieurs* no longer risked losing their hats for a glimpse of her *chatte* although only instants before, or so it seems, so many had leaned precariously close to the stage. How many silk hats has she sent soaring above the dressed supper tables and later, after her own supper, how many times has she seen a trouser fly hastily unbuttoned and a cock, its dressed head as violet as her own deep vulva, greet her with a wink? How many cocks leaping into her *chatte* as through a hoop of fire? The bright jewels tossed at her feet, the crisp violet cash rolled like cigars and pressed to her palm. Her armoires brimming with bright slippers sewn of glazed leather.

But now La Goulue is old and fat. To make a go of it, she has sold her plates, her knives and bracelets, the red petticoats and the bloomers slit so that when one kicks off a hat, one's *chatte* may size up the clientele. She has bought a weary tribe of misused animals as long in tooth as is she, and their cages and a gypsy wagon, its planking in need of paint—which is where we now sit.

The animals—one bear, four lions, a black panther, and a hyena—she keeps in her yard, just outside the old walls of Paris. At night she can hear the heart of Paris beating without her. She knows that those who loved her are themselves retired or in the last throes of an affair with a girl whose eye-catching beauty can do nothing to stop the pocket watch set out upon the bedside table mocking the moments as they pass. And she recalls how when she ordered duck at the Maison Dorée, the carver—he was dressed like a bridegroom—would debone it for her, and serve the flesh in sixty perfect slices arranged like a fan. On a plate of fine *faïence*, she tells me, painted with the green figures of Chinamen, and other curious things. The duck's fresh blood in a pewter pitcher to keep it from clotting, and stirred into the sauce. Cherries on fire, tumbling after.

The animals' food she makes with stale bread she haggles for, using what remains of her charm. The beasts, she reminds the bakers, the restaurant cooks, the neighbors—are like us. They must eat! (She does not give them bones to gum for fear of rousing old appetites; her beasts' nostalgia for better days is as great as her own.) Every afternoon when she returns to her little scruffy yard and its cages, its piles of straw—one clean, one very dirty—her sack rattles with stale baguettes.

Her lions have all lost their teeth, as has the poor bear who, like his mistress, can no longer stir a crowd. But the panther . . . now that's another story.

On tour in the early spring, the panther had torn off a child's arm. The boy leaning far too close to the cage, wanting to *pet the kitty*. La Goulue wiggles her bare fingers in my face. She has sold the last of her rings to pay the surgeon's fees. "It is fortunate," she tells me, "the child is not a girl. Ladies love to soothe a man who has suffered such misadventures whereas *ces messieurs* will settle for nothing less than perfect beauty." I nod and accept the cup of verbena she offers along with a slice of toast thickly frosted with her own quince jam. "The cat-meat man," she sighs, "comes for the panther tomorrow."

If on a winter's morning you elect to spend time with La Goulue, she makes you feel at home. (I, for one, have always been susceptible to the nostalgia of others.) Her hospitality, her vivacity, her full bosom bring to mind the great aunt or grandmother one adored, whose infrequent visits were enlivened by indiscretions and gifts of tinned sweets. To tell the truth, the afternoon I spent with her, those brief, sweet moments, have left an odd impression, for looking back I see myself as a boy of ten or so and this not just because of her tales and her toast, but the fact that she presses stereoviews upon me, views of herself strolling the gardens of Versailles in a dress of the palest lavender, and again, in that same dress, standing among the fountains of St. Petersburg. And there is another hand-tinted view of the dancer in her prime, slender in camisole and drawers, straddling one of the bronze lions that guard the Spanish throne.

"You see how I was fated for lions from the start," she laughs, and squeezes my wrist as though I were a favorite nephew. And she tells me how the waiter at the Maison Dorée debones her duck in a trice, how the dwarf Lautrec entertains her and her friends with an erotic patter so hilarious it is all she can do to keep herself from pissing on her velvet chair.

"For you see," she continues, "in those brief years, appetite ruled our lives. My *chatte* kept Paris hot and lively, whereas now even my lions are geriatric, the hyena too irritable to roll over and offer her belly for a scratch, the panther doomed. My yard," she smiles sadly, "reeks of feral creatures in idleness." And she yawns. She is wanting her nap.

As we walk towards the front gate, she pulls her stiff underwear piece by piece from the line and says philosophically:

"Don't worry about me, *Monsieur*. You see: it is only natural for meteors to fall from the sky."

When I leave La Goulue—and it is late in the day—the first winter thunderstorm strikes just as I reach the street. The rainy season is fairly set in Paris, and thunder, lightning, and heavy storms are common both night and day. When after midnight the clouds disperse, the stars peer down through the spare foliage of the pollarded trees, and one may see the ardent face of the moon as volatile as smoke.

GRÉGOIRE BOUILLIER

PERCIVAL EVERETT

GRÉGOIRE BOUILLIER

❖

Anything will do today to get your mind on something else.
To play for time. Dissolve the memory of her chestnut smile,
her tiny little breasts and distraught gaze. Since she finally
got married to someone else. To the guy she already called
her fiancé when you first met her: a hopeless situation. One
day he told her: "You can't leave me, your parents like me
too much." That's surely what's called a "sledgehammer
argument"; but now you're the one who's been hit with a
ton of bricks, who sees the stars, knowing you'll have to hold
your peace forever, as the saying goes; and, be that as it may,
for months you've been spending an enormous amount of
energy trying to blot out of your memory that one particularly radiant night when she embraced you, whispered in
your ear that she loved you, and then promptly fainted in
your arms, sliding down your body like a sack and spread-
ing slowly out at your feet; there you were in the street and
she wouldn't wake up, even though you slapped her in the
face and so did the paramedics; she had to be taken to the
emergency room, she was in a coma for three hours (an alco-
hol-induced coma, the intern noted, though of course that
was but a miniscule part of the truth). Yes, for months you've
been trying hard to climb back on the horse, to gather your
strength, to tear down your crazy castles in the air one by
one, to re-plant the forest that you kept missing because
of the trees, to retrieve the bathwater with the baby and,

finally, to milk the ram, second by second, minute by minute, as though every new hour represented the only frontier still attainable. As though each hour was a battle to be waged against nothingness (an exhausting endeavor), until finally you'd put some distance between you and her, a distance which you could one day call oblivion. You haven't reached that stage yet. The truth of that unspeakable love still escapes you and your bafflement never gives you any respite—for example, you now change your shoes every day, you can't help yourself, you can't wear the same pair of shoes for two days in a row, a problem you never had before; it even got to the point where you caught yourself changing shoes twice in one afternoon, and this incomprehensible dandyism suddenly stared you in the face, yes, you suddenly realized this weird and ridiculous new obsession was your way of telling the world you hadn't found the shoes that fit, in other words, a suitable match, and this was now a disaster that had taken on alarming, in fact pathological proportions in your case. That's the way it is. It isn't the first time you've had this kind of misadventure. But this time the truth of this never-ending love completely escapes you, actually everything escapes you, even when you're shopping in the supermarket, talking about sports, courting a girl, or reading a newspaper (awful period). For instance, yesterday you came across a flyer that had been taped up on the subway platform and you instantly felt a kind of howl rise up from your entire being when you read it; they were searching for "Grégoire, an autistic boy last seen in the subway on September 23, 2006," dressed in blue jeans and a white *"Les Colombages"* T-shirt, and as you looked around anxiously you wondered whether you didn't have a white T-shirt marked *"Les Colombages"* in your closet, and then how long would it take them to find you? And what state would you be in? What passageways would you be wandering down? Worn away by what people? With shoes or without? One thing is certain: all is not lost, since someone cares about your disappearance; you almost called the number on the flyer then and there to set their minds at rest and ask them to come and get you. The day before yesterday, you saw an item in the paper that put you on edge: in the suburbs someone had hanged his dog (a seven-year-old female Labrador) from the balcony of his house because his wife had left him; all day long, whenever anyone spoke to you, you found yourself barking back. Yes, every day you take any event, no matter how inconsequential, as an occasion to tug at the thread of your own existence, hoping to uncover the underlying pattern. With the aim of exploring the immense swindle your life has become—and which life in general is. It occurs to you this has always been a way you had of overcoming loneliness, the world's more hilarious twists and turns, and the certitude that no one will die in your place. Neither the Pope nor Percival Everett, no, no one will die in your place and no one will live in your place, if you can really call this living. Not even the proverbial Cassius in the syllogism no matter how many times you prove he's mortal. And certainly not Günter Grass. To justify the belated confession of his brief and youthful Nazi past, you read (this was on a Monday, on the terrace of a café) that he first felt he had to "find the literary form to tell the truth." In other words, you worked it out in your head, it took some sixty years. You sighed. Put down the newspaper. Looked around for something, anything that could focus the inexpressible feeling suddenly overwhelming you. Like a wind coming from the South sweeping up everything in its path, and especially the word "novel." A girl was walking by. You followed her with your eyes without thinking. She moved with a sway, that anatomically miraculous hip effect which only women have a knack for, though not all women. At the same time, you kept repeating to yourself mentally, "find the literary form to tell the truth," "find the literary form to tell the truth" . . . All of a sudden it occurred to you that this might be another way of saying, "find the shoes that fit." You sprang up and, driven by a sudden impulse, almost a feeling of jubilation, you followed close on the heels of the girl. Who knows if, as she walked, she wasn't also writing something important with her feet, something you could read on the asphalt by connecting her steps. It was a silly idea, even vaguely mystical, but the only way you could think of to express the immutable absurdity of everything.

Translated by Catherine Temerson

PERCIVAL EVERETT

❖

And as you walked in her steps it became apparent that you were no more following her than she was leading you. You and she were simply tracing the same path, the same lines the same text, punctuating each turn of a corner or glance at a shop window with a question mark or a comma, but never a period. The period, that dimensionless position in space, without depth, without extension, but able to bring assertion to an abrupt halt, to pause meaning in its tracks. You walked in those steps, hers or not hers, and wondered who walked in those very steps behind you. A boy in a familiar T-shirt? A Labrador retriever? A boy walking a retriever, the collar too tight for the dog's neck? Future lovers? Current lovers? Past lovers? Or that one past lover? Yes, she was walking behind you that day, observing the treads of your shoes, waiting for them to change, to become new shoes, different shoes, different feet and finally different steps and then you stopped, let the girl whose trail you were tracing fade from sight across a bridge and you looked back, thinking of Eurydice and of course she was not there. She was not there because you looked back, your looking back necessarily erasing her from the scene. You walked to the middle of the bridge and looked down at the blackness of the water and realized that it could be many hundreds of feet deep or mere inches and that either way it made no difference, as the depth of few things makes any real difference.

Then you looked down at your feet, at the boots that had worn ever slightly over the meters of sidewalk, leaving part of them and bringing along part of the city. The boots must be changed, you thought, and then with every step as you left the bridge the foot appearing in front of you wore a different shoe. A slip-on with a padded collar, leather upper, and rubber sole. An unconstructed rubber-soled Oxford with red lace. A nubuck leather avocado and taupe sneaker with a synthetic lining. An ankle-high boot with fleur-de-lis design accents, leather upper and rubber sole. An all-leather loafer with a laser-etched design on the vamp. A square-toed double-zip leather boot with a buckle in the back. Step after step, right foot, left foot, right, left, shoe after shoe, each one ill-fitting. The knuckles of your toes were rubbed raw, bleeding, peeling, reminding you of every step and of all your steps, taken and yet to be taken. And all of this because you couldn't shake her words confessing love from your head. You stopped then in front of a shoe shop, stared through the glass at all of the spanking new shoes and found also your reflection. You entered and the woman who worked there asked you a reasonable question, "May I help you?"

You looked at her and said the most reasonable thing you'd said in years. You said, "I'd like some shoes that fit."

PHILIPPE CLAUDEL

ALEKSANDAR HEMON

PHILIPPE CLAUDEL

STILL LIFE

❖

We drive for hours on the endless black ribbons of our suburban freeways. Slowly, in a way so perfectly synchronized that at times we appear to be imprisoned in toy cars on an electric track, our course and speed governed by no will of our own but by some higher invisible hand.

For the most part it is dark when we leave and when we return. We never see the faces of the other drivers whose vehicles sometimes whisk past with a soft rumble. All the roads are alike; and all lead to the same places.

We live in green suburbs and our elegant houses are barely visible through the large trees—the cedars, sycamores, poplars and oaks that protect them and also tend to smother them. Our houses are vast, calm, and silent. Their façades of painted wood, white marble, or red brick create a peaceful feeling, a feeling of security, of the permanence of things.

If, as rarely happens, we linger there during morning hours, when we would normally be at work in the metal-and-glass towers that hold our offices, we are suddenly invaded by a calming thought: We never experience our houses like this. In the clear light of day they are like sleeping animals, cuddled in a magnificent lethargy, a stone-bound coma that puts some of us in mind of sarcophagi: massive tombs lined up close together, as if for mutual reassurance.

We do not know our neighbors. We assume that their lives are just like ours, circumscribed by the work that takes up all our time. We could speak to them—for they are very close by, separated from us only by the branches of the great trees that the wind moves from time to time and that the autumn strips bare—but we never do. We hear no sound from their direction, not the slightest vibration, just as no doubt they hear nothing from us.

Each weekend we have friends over. We organize dinner parties that are never fully attended because our houses are hard to find—many of our guests get lost, for the streets are all alike, and poorly lit. Our four-figure house numbers are bewildering. In the night people lose their bearings. And the freeway eats up hours. Our friends never stay late; they need to get back to their own houses, far away and just like ours. We laugh heartily. We talk of books, sculpture exhibitions, and work. We drink fine wines and admire the labels on the bottles. We play at being happy. We kiss when we part.

We leave bedside lights, sconces, chandeliers, and night-lights on at all times, even when we are gone. Perhaps we want to feel that our houses are alive even when we are away from them—and therefore that we are alive as well. When we get back in the evening, the houses are bathed in warm light, and the sofas, the carpets, the beds, and the hangings and pictures on the walls seem to welcome us, as if inviting us back into a conversation we had been having the night before.

We each have a swimming pool, a deck, a gym, and a gardener who comes twice a week to rake leaves, filter the water for the pool, and trim the lawn with geometric precision. We never know his name. If now and again we happen to look at his face, we may notice that he has changed, that this is not the same man as last time, but it makes no difference: the yard work is always done with admirable consistency and precision.

Our children grow up in faraway schools and colleges. Every day we read messages from them on computer screens that also show their faces. They send us greetings, tender platitudes, and we reply in kind. We do not miss them.

In our city centers the streets are deserted, abandoned to winds that pick up speed and violence in the canyons between the great towers. In the middle of the day pedestrians are rarely seen; after dark, our televisions tell us, murders and rapes take place amidst a population of poor people that we never encounter. In the morning, however, there is no blood to be seen.

Our houses are sparkling clean. Nothing is left lying about. While we are out, cleaning ladies push state-of-the-art vacuum cleaners, wash our dishes and tableware, make our beds, clean our windows, and polish our parquet floors. In the evening, after the sun has set—although we have barely seen it through the tinted glass of our office buildings—we leave our offices in a state of mild disorder which by next morning will have vanished.

We are not rich, but we have money, and do nothing with it. We love women and men whose features we have never seen but with whom we conduct electronic correspondences in which we tell them the ways we would like to penetrate, caress, and touch them. We no longer make love to our partners.

Sometimes we watch them sleep. On occasion, too, we touch them tenderly, or find words that remind us how we used to be, before, long ago, when our life together was just beginning. But these moments produce no nostalgia.

We ask ourselves very few questions.

We surrender ourselves to the succession of days.

We make sure not to stop and think.

We speak to one another as little as possible.

We never think of death.

At night we place masks over our eyes to sleep.

We like the darkness they bring, covering our eyelids like a velvet palm.

We slip into sleep, then at last we are no longer ourselves.

Translated by Donald Nicholson-Smith

ALEKSANDAR HEMON

GOOD LIVING

❖

Back in the days of the war in Bosnia, I was surviving in
Chicago by selling magazine subscriptions door-to-door.
My employers thought that my Bosnian accent, clearly
manufactured in the nether area of *other cultures,* was quirky,
and therefore a stimulant to the shopping instincts of
suburban Americans. I was desperate at the time, what with
the war and displacement, so I shamelessly exploited any
smidgen of pity I could detect in lonely housewives and
grumpy retirees whose doors I knocked at. Many of them
were excited by my very presence at their doorstep, as I was
living evidence of the American dream: here I was overcoming adverse circumstances in a new country, much like
the forebears of the future subscriber, presently signing the
check and wistfully relating the epic saga of the ancestral
transition to America.

But I had much too much of a dramatic foreign
accent for the prime subscription-selling turf of the North
Shore suburbs, where people, quaintly smothered by the
serenity of wealth, regularly read *Numismatic News* and
bought a lifetime subscription to *Life Extension.* Instead, I was
deployed in the working-class suburbs, bordered with steel-
mill complexes and landfills, and populated with people
who, unlike the denizens of North Shore, did not think

that I coveted what they had, because they did not exactly want it themselves.

My best turf was Blue Island, way down Western Avenue, where addresses had five-digit numbers, as though the town was far in the back of the long line of people waiting to enter downtown paradise. I got along pretty well with the Blue Islanders. They could quickly recognize the indelible lousiness of my job; they offered me food and water; once I nearly got laid. They did not waste their time contemplating the purpose of human life; their years were spent as a tale is told: slowly, steadily approaching the inexorable end. In the meantime, all they wanted was to live, wisely use what little love they had accrued, and endure it all with the anesthetic help of television and magazines. I happened to be in their neighborhood to offer the magazines.

A smokestack of the garbage incinerator, complete with sparks flying upward, loomed over the town like a church spire. Perhaps that was why the deciduous leaves in Blue Island died so abundantly and beautifully, its streets thickly covered with yellow, orange, ochre, russet layers. One day I walked over a dry carpet of honey-colored leaves, up to a dusty porch littered with disintegrating coupon sheets. A brushy black cat did not move as I walked by; a wooden figure of Virgin Mary hung stiffly by the bell. Someone shouted: "Come in!" before I rang, and in I walked, into a cavernous dark room reeking of overcurdled milk and beeswax tapers. On the couch in its center sat a small priest—the solemn attire, the white collar, the silver-cross pendant—his toy feet barely reaching the floor. His face and bald dome were blighted with red blotches and flaking skin. In his right hand, he had a glass of Scotch, the half-full bottle on the coffee table in front of him surrounded by the rubble of newspapers and snack bags. On his potbelly ledge, around the cross, there were potato-chip crumbles.

"What can I do you for?" he said and belched. "Excuse me. What can I do for you?" He pointed at the armchair across the coffee table, so I sat down.

A salesman's job largely consists of mindless repetition of prefabricated phrases. Thus I offered him a wide selection of magazines that covered all areas of contemporary living. There was a magazine for everyone, whether his interest be in astronomy or self-betterment or gardening. I could also offer a wide variety of titles for a contemporary Christian reader: *Christian Today, Christian Professional, God's Word Today* . . .

"Where're you from?" he asked and took a large sip from the glass. The color of the Scotch rhymed with the leaves outside.

"Bosnia."

"Be not forgetful to entertain strangers," he slurred, "thereby some have entertained angels unawares."

I nodded and suggested some magazines that would open new horizons for him in archeology or medicine or science. He shook his head, frowning, as though he could not believe in my existence.

"Have you lost anyone close to you in the war? Anyone you loved?"

"Some," I said, and lowered my head, suggesting intense soul pain.

"It must have been hard for you."

"It hasn't been easy."

Abruptly he turned his head toward the dark door in the back of the room and yelled: "Michael! Michael! Come here and see someone who is really suffering. Come and meet an actual human being."

Michael stepped into the room buttoning up, the impeccably white shirt closing in on a chest smooth and hairless.

He was blonde and blue-eyed, incongruously handsome in the Blue-Island dreariness, sporting a square jaw of an American movie star.

"The young man here is from Bosnia. Do you have any idea where Bosnia is, Michael?"

Michael said nothing and strolled over to the coffee table, throwing his shoulders model-like. He dug up a cigarette from the coffee table wreckage and walked out leaving a wake of anger behind.

"He smokes," the priest said, plaintively. "He breaks my heart."

"Smoking is bad," I said.

"But he works out a lot," the priest said. "Absent in spirit, but present in body."

I had a selection of magazines just for Michael, I said. *Men's Health, Shape, Self, Body and Soul*, all of them covering a wide range of interests: workout regimes, fitness tips, diets, etc.

"Michael!" the priest hollered. "Would you like a subscription to *Body and Soul*?"

"Fuck you," Michael screamed back.

The priest finished his Scotch and pushed himself awkwardly up from the couch to reach the bottle. I was tempted to help him.

"If there were a magazine called Selfishness," he grumbled, "Michael would be editor in chief."

He refilled the glass and returned into the depth of the couch. He scratched his dome and a flock of skin flakes fluttered up in its orbit.

"Michael wants to be an actor, you see. He is nothing if not vanity and vexation," the priest said. "But he has only managed to be a fluffer in an odd adult movie. And to tell you the truth, I cannot see a future in fluffing for him."

It was time for me to go. I was experienced enough to recognize the commencement of an unsolicited confession. I had stood up and left in the middle of a confession before—no doubt adding to the confessor's flow of tears—because it had been a prudent thing to do. But I could not leave this time, perhaps because the drama was titillatingly unresolved, or because the priest was so minuscule and weak, whole parchments peeling off of his forehead. Having been often pitied, I savored pitying someone else.

"I've known Michael since he was a boy. But now he thinks he can go off on his own. It is not good that the man shall be alone, it is not good."

Michael appeared out of the room in the back, his hair immaculately combed but still quivering in exasperation. He stormed past us and left the house, slamming the door behind him.

The priest finished off the Scotch in the glass in one big gulp.

"We all do fade as a leaf," he said and threw the glass toward the coffee table. It dropped on the top of the mess, and rolled down, off the table, out of sight. It was time for me to go; I started getting up.

"Do you know who Saint Thomas Aquinas was?" he said, raising his finger, as though about to preach. "When he was a young man, his family did not want him to devote his life to the Church so they sent a beautiful maiden to tempt him out of it. And he chased her away with a torch."

He stared at me for a very long moment, as though waiting for a confirmation of my understanding, but it never came—understanding was not my job.

"Be not righteous *overmuch*," he said, fumbling the word overmuch. "I never had a torch."

The door flung open and Michael charged back in. I sunk into the chair, as he walked to the priest and stood above him, pointing the finger at him, shaking it, his jaw jutted sideways with fury.

"I just want to say one thing, you sick fuck," he said, a few loose hairs stuck to his sweaty brow. "I just want to say one more thing to you."

We waited in the overwhelming silence, the priest closing his eyes, as though anticipating a punch. But Michael could not think of one more thing to say, so he finally said nothing, turned on his heel and marched out, not bothering to slam the door this time. The priest grabbed a couch pillow and started banging it against his forehead, howling and hissing in pain. I took the opportunity to tiptoe toward the open door.

"Wait," he wailed. "I want to subscribe. I want subscription. Wait a minute."

So I signed him up for two plum two-year sub- scriptions. His name was Father James McMahon. For the rest of the evening, I went around the neighborhood, telling everybody—the old ladies, the young mothers, the cranky ex-policemen—that Father McMahon had just subscribed to *American Woodworker* and *Good Living*, wouldn't you know it? A few asked me how he seemed to be doing, and I would tell them that he had a big fight with his young friend. And they would sigh and say: "Is that so?" and frown and subscribe to *Creative Knitting* and *Family Fun*. It was by far my best day as a magazine salesman. At the end of the shift, waiting to be picked up by the turf manager, I watched the flickering of TV lights in the windows and the sparkling stars up in the sky, and I thought: I could live here. I could live here forever. This is a good place for me.

LUC LANG

JOHN EDGAR WIDEMAN

LUC LANG

INITIATION

❖

I choose, as always, the emus' area (members of the ratite family), down below the path, the one closed off not by a fence, but by a sod-covered ditch, the brown beasts and their long bluish necks able to sniff up at the top of the grassy gap, at foot level of the passing visitors . . . the young children gladly stop here with parents or grandparents . . . when one of these kids remains within reach of the emus, fascinated by these ostrich-like heads, black feathers, orange eyes and penetrating stares . . . I step closer to the ditch, a few yards from the child, trample on the grassy embankment, pull out a tuft of grass and offer it, conspicuously, to the nearest emu . . . who greedily devours it, asks for more . . .

. . . no, rarely visit the mammals, rather take care of the feathered creatures: ashen cranes, marabous, flamingoes, birds of prey, parakeets, macaws, cockatoos, not going to list them all, the zoo houses a wide variety of species…clean the aviary, distribute grains, fruits and raw vegetables, blocks of lard and all sorts of things, take care of each one, yes, it's been 23 years, working amid the usual chirping exchanges, yes, among the same parakeets and parrots: Hail to you, O Jack! The top of the morning to you, Lucas noble sir! . . . I love this grandiloquence in birds! and twenty seconds later, as a way of engaging the conversation, as in an eternal ritual, "you know you have beautiful dreams, don't you?" . . . which is not true! birds have vague bits of barely sketched dreams, and I, with the passing years, no longer dream at all! eyes wide open in the darkness of my sleepless nights . . . who cares! "you know you have beautiful dreams, don't you?" used to work like a dog trying to teach them this . . . in fact, it was: "you know you have a beautiful gleam, don't you?" because parrots live to be so old . . . still be here the day I retire . . . "you know you have beautiful dreams, don't you?" ah!!! the fury those first times . . . why do you say *dreams?* It's *gleam!* according to the zoo's veterinarian, an expert in the phonetics of speaking birds, they have real difficulty articulating diphthongs, triphthongs and gutturals: such as: *g*leam, *g*uillotine, *g*uts, *k*eelhauling, mus*k*eteer, *c*orsair . . . on the other hand, the coronal alveolars: d, l, r, s, such as: *d*ream, *Sl*oop, Va*l*paraiso, pi*r*ate are child's play for them, they who don't have lips or vocal cords . . . it's their respiratory system! the renowned syrinx at the intersection of two bronchi that allows them to inflect so many sounds and syllables, said the vet poet . . . in the end, *dreams* is more joyful than *gleam*, more uplifting, more charged with a future, brings back the time when I imagined taking off for marine and tropical horizons, flown over by multicolored birds . . . but there you have it, stayed put in a temperate climate, amid Parisian vegetation, among cement boulders where I earned the right to live among birds from five continents with whom I'm finishing out my days . . .

. . . getting back to the emus (one of the closest descendants of dinosaurs!) to whom I give a tuft of grass six steps away from the astounded kid . . . nothing is more tempting to a young child than feeding an animal . . . an irresistible urge underlies this gesture, to feed, to tame, to become the privileged interlocutor, the intimate friend of a nature until now silent and indomitable, to discover in it his own humanity—in short—to repeat the movement of ancient man who domesticated nature and inhabits it in his imaginary universe, millenniums of work buried in our reptilian brain that the child tirelessly replays . . . so, it's his turn to pull up a tuft of grass, often it's his parents who do it for him, he grabs the tuft, awkwardly, between his tender little fingers, it's at this moment that I stand back up, ready to nonchalantly distance myself . . . the little kid extends his miniscule hand towards the emu's head which quickly bows with sinewy neck movements akin to the dance of a snake, opens his powerful beak, and . . . chomp! violently pinches the unsuspecting fingers of the frail pale hand, cuts till it's bleeding the open pulp of one, two, or three fingers, inevitably, given the internal structure of the bird's beak . . . terror, tears, pain, blood pissing everywhere, smiles erased, child traumatized, parents pallid and distraught, happiness turned to dust, turning my back to them, leaving slowly to attend to my work, a troubled smile of contentment on my lips, irrepressible . . . you don't put your hand out in any old way! as if the world were at his disposal! no! reality! a lesson in reality! the end of dreams! I giggle inside . . . this morning, under a blinding sun, the 386th victim . . . and the mother who comes after me, hunting me down: but, your uniform! yes, forest green! you . . . yes you! you belong to the zoo! yes, body and soul! to the birds, yes! . . . this is the example you give! on purpose? so that my son gets bit! You bastard! I've spotted you! going to report you! . . . slammed the metal service door of the lemurs' boulder in her face . . . off limits to the public, you crazy woman!

Translated by A. Kaiser

JOHN EDGAR WIDEMAN

WOLF WHISTLE

❖

At first I think it's a mad boy let out of the attic or basement for air an hour a day whistling at me from the rear of a long yard, a demented boy unfamiliar with skin darker than his but crazy enough not to be afraid, not to care, and whistling scorn, racial epithets, his shrill keening anger at being surprised, intruded upon by a trespasser black as the devil or *ooh-la-la*, cutie-pie, what the fuck do we have here, sweetie, shrieked loud enough for the whole neighborhood to enjoy in the long silence of Le Moustoir at the eastern lip of Arradon on the Gulf of Morbihan in the vicinity of Vannes in Brittany in France in Western Europe in a Universe with ample space to incarcerate boys in Turkish-looking, rusty cages crowned with minarets, hung on trees, two of them, two cages um-brellaed by trees at the front of the long yard belonging to a house on the corner of rue Saint Martin and rue de la Touline I passed without seeing on daily walks to the part tavern, part grocery store or morning strolls to the closest sea or jog-ging five kilometers to Toulandac that opens like a tourist's postcard dream when you turn a corner and coast parallel to the coastline, Ile aux Moines, a gray lump framed in endless blue distance by the long, slow smile of curve embracing double-deck ferries, white sails, striped sails, a sailing school with pennants flapping where kids try to learn to fly like fish and birds, a convincing advertisement for the good life, a trick, achieved with mirrors, even though happy, piping voices reach me there, all the way up there on a road above Toulandac when I glide or pretend to glide invisibly, effortlessly as wind towards the fence-lined path that cuts steep and straight down to the beach, to acres of naked flesh, rocks and rocks and rocks, large as elephants, tiny as stinging gnats, families packed on weekends into this small, select space with stunning views almost to open sea, sea a bright lawn of water barely rippling as it laps the beach whose gently sloping sandy bottom remains visible underwater, many steps from shore, the footing awkwardly rocky through knee-high puddles of nodding algae, but soon smooth enough except for stones sharp as nails, blue, chilling water shallow for youngsters to wade far, far out, clear and calm, never a black triangle of fin crossing parallel to the horizon, no pain till you step out shivering, blue, slit open, the kids can play while you half watch, half doze, stupid in the sun, no need ever to get your feet wet or cold again, gashed again, your mad boy free a minute or two in the yard to wolf whistle or coo or cackle at Le Moustoir neighbors passing by, at children from the kindergarten across rue Saint Martin who break out early afternoons to car doors slamming them in, their young mothers waiting naked and dazed as sunbathers or hiding in drab colors of little donut cars jammed in the shade of trees adjacent to the house with a long yard on the corner where if I could ever get its attention, if I could ever master its language or the French language it might bi-lingually understand, I would teach one of the parrots or the other to be a mad boy again, not so mad he's locked in a cage but mad enough to whistle and hoot horribly obscene, scary things at kids and their mothers, warning them about the bright razor sea you can smell from here and all the dead things in it, including pale skin of mothers burnt to ash, including children set out to play, set out nonchalantly

72

like they're turned out to play in traffic on busy streets of this Universe shaped like a long yard from whose shadowy rear-end a hoarse, mocking, insane voice chops at me, cuts my legs from under me so I never make it to Toulandac one day, just kneel here, bleed here, outside the house's white stucco, chin high wall, begging forgiveness of a boy born mad and almost mute but he's picked up the gift of assaulting others with a few choice, nasty noises picked up from his Universe, on my knees imploring him to forgive me for blaming and cursing him because I saw for the first time two parrots staring, swaying, pecking gently at the bars of their rusted, oriental cages, two lynched birds I'd teach to warble *Emmett Till, Emmett Till* if I could, but they just sit there preening, ruffling their ratty feathers, each twin nailed to its perch, neither one making a sound in response to my coaxing, my artless imitations of them and I give up.

CONTRIBUTORS

Esther Allen's translation of Antonio Muñoz Molina's novella *In Her Absence* is coming out from Other Press in 2007. She is Executive Director of the Center for Literary Translation at Columbia University, and the author of an International PEN report on translation and globalization. In 2006 she was named Chevalier de l'ordre des arts et des lettres by the French Ministry of Culture and Communication.

Grégoire Bouillier was born in 1960. He recently published *L'invité mystère* (Allia, 2004) which came out in the U.S. as *The Mystery Guest* (Farrar, Straus and Giroux, 2006). His first book, *Rapport sur moi* (Allia 2002, Prix de Flore 2002), is in the process of being translated by Houghton Mifflin under the title *Report on Myself*.

Robert Olen Butler has published fourteen works of fiction in English, eight of which have been translated into French. His most recent was a book of 62 very short stories in the voices of decapitated heads, entitled *Severance* (Chronicle Books, 2006), which appeared in France as *Mots de tête* (Rivages, 2005). He won the Pulitzer Prize for Fiction in 1993.

Philippe Claudel was born in 1962 in France. He teaches literature at the University of Nancy. He has recently published *Le monde sans les enfants* (Stock, 2006) and his novel *Les âmes grises* (Stock, 2003) was published in the U.S. by Knopf Publishing in 2006 under the title *By a Slow River*.

Marie Darrieussecq was born in 1969 in Bayonne, France. She has recently published *Zoo* (P.O.L., 2006). All her seven novels are published in France by P.O.L. and in London by Faber and Faber. *Pig Tales* (1998), *My Phantom Husband* (1999), and *Undercurrents* (2000) were published in the U.S. by The New Press.

Rikki Ducornet is the author of seven novels including *The Jade Cabinet* (Dalkey Archive Press, 1992), finalist for the National Book Critics' Circle Award. She received the Lannan Literary Award for Fiction in 2004. She recently published a collection of short stories, *The Word Desire* (Dalkey Archive Press, 2005) and *Gazelle* (Knopf, 2003) was published in France by Joëlle Losfeld (2007).

Percival Everett is Distinguished Professor of English at the University of Southern California. His most recent books include *American Desert* (Hyperion, 2004), *Damned If I Do* (Graywolf Press, 2004) and *Wounded* (Graywolf Press, 2005). His novel *The Water Cure* will be published by Graywolf Press in the fall of 2007. His novels are published in France by Actes Sud.

Bilingual novelist and poet **Raymond Federman** was born in 1928 in France, but resides in the U.S. He recently published *My Body in Nine Parts* (Starcherone Books, 2005), *Return to Manure* (FC2/University of Alabama Press, 2006), *A qui de droit*, and *Le livre de Sam* (both with Al Dante, 2006).

Aleksandar Hemon was born in Sarajevo in 1964. He is the author of *Question of Bruno* (Doubleday, 2000) and *Nowhere Man* (Doubleday, 2002). His novels are published in France by Robert Laffont.

Jeanine Herman lives in New York City. Her translation of Julien Gracq's *Reading Writing* was recently published by Turtle Point Press. She is currently translating a novel by Eric Laurrent, *Do Not Touch*, for Dalkey Archive Press (published in France by Minuit).

Born in Indonesia in 1936, educated in the Netherlands, and residing in the U.S. since 1958, **Marjolijn de Jager** translates fiction, non-fiction, and poetry from both the French and the Dutch. Her "specialty" area is Francophone African literature, particularly women authors. She has won several awards, including a NEA Translation Grant for poetry (2005).

A. Kaiser is a translator of French and Spanish and a member of the PEN American Center Translation Committee. She was coordinator of translations and translator for the project *To My American Readers* (2006) as well as for this 2007 project, *As You Were Saying*. She holds degrees in political science (U.S.) and comparative literature (France).

Luc Lang was born in 1956. He teaches aesthetics at L'Ecole Nationale Supérieure des Beaux-Arts de Paris et Cergy. He has recently published *La fin des paysages* (Stock, 2006) and his novel *Strange Ways* was published in English by Phoenix House (London) in 2002.

Camille Laurens was born in 1957 in Dijon. She taught in Normandy and in Morocco. She has recently published *Ni toi ni moi* (P.O.L., 2006). Her novel *Dans ces bras-là* (P.O.L, 2000), which was awarded the Prix Femina, was published in the U.S. by Random House in 2004 as *In His Arms*.

Rick Moody was born in 1961 in New York City. His most recent publications are *The Black Veil* (Little, Brown and Company, 2003) and *The Diviners* (Little, Brown and Company, 2005), as well as the forthcoming collection of novellas, *Right Livelihoods* (Little, Brown and Company, June 2007). His books are published in France by Rivages and L'Olivier.

Donald Nicholson-Smith's translations include works by Guy Debord, Jean Piaget, Jean-Patrick Manchette, Paco Ignacio Taibo II, J.-B. Pontalis and Jean Laplanche, Thierry Jonquet, Henri Lefebvre, and Raoul Vaneigem. Born in Manchester, England, he is a long-time resident of New York City. At present he is at work on Guillaume Apollinaire's love-and-war letters from the trenches of World War I and on some of Antonin Artaud's last writings.

Jacques Roubaud was born in 1932 in Caluire et Cuire (France). Now retired, he was a director of studies at the Ecole des Hautes Etudes en Sciences Sociales (EHESS). He has recently published *Nous, les moins-que-rien, fils ainés de personne, multiroman* (Fayard, 2006) and his book *The Form of a City Changes Faster, Alas, Than the Human Heart,* was published in the U.S. by Dalkey Archive Press in 2006.

Born in France of an Andalusian father and Catalonian mother, **Lydie Salvayre** studied medicine in Toulouse and specialised in psychiatry. She is the author of over ten works, translated into fourteen languages, of which the English versions include *The Award* (Four Walls Eight Windows, 1997), *The Lecture* (Dalkey Archive Press, 2005), *The Company of Ghosts* (Dalkey Archive Press, 2006) and *Everyday Life* (Dalkey Archive Press, 2006). In France her books are published by Le Seuil (*La méthode Mila,* 2005) and Verticales.

Catherine Temerson has an M. A. degree in Russian literature from Harvard University and a Ph.D. in Comparative Literature from New York University. She has worked in film and theater, taught language and literature, authored books in French, and translated over a dozen books. Her most recent translation is Florence Noiville's *Isaac B. Singer, A Life* (Stock, 2003/Farrar, Straus & Giroux, 2006).

Alyson Waters teaches literary translation in the French Department at Yale University and is the Managing Editor of *Yale French Studies.* Her most recent book-length translations are Reda Bensmaïa's *Experimental Nations, Or: The Invention of the Maghreb* (Princeton UP, 2003) and Vassilis Alexakis's *Foreign Words* (Stock, 2002/Autumn Hill Books, 2006), for which she received a National Endowment for the Arts Translation Fellowship in 2004. She lives in Brooklyn, NY.

John Edgar Wideman was born in 1941 in Washington, D.C. He recently published *Two Cities* (Houghton Mifflin Company, 1998), *Hoop Roots: Basketball, Race and Love* (Houghton Mifflin Company, 2001), and *God's Gym: Stories* (Houghton Mifflin Company, 2005). His books are published in France by Gallimard.

The Cultural Services of the French Embassy in the
United States, the PEN American Center, and the Center
for Literary Translation at Columbia University

present

FRENCH VOICES

French Voices is a translation program designed to assist
the U.S. publication of 30 books written in French and
published after 2000.

The series will offer English-language readers a new
Francophone perspective on our globalized world.

Thirty books will be selected by a committee of French
and American book industry professionals.

Each American publisher of these books will receive a
grant of $6,000 to help cover the cost of translation.

A short preface by a well-known writer will introduce
each book, and a reading guide will be available free at
www.frenchbooknews.com.

For further information, please visit:

www.frenchbooknews.com

FRENCH
VOICES
FRENCH
VOICES

THE VILLA GILLET QUESTIONS TODAY'S WORLD

The Villa Gillet is a research centre devoted
to contemporary art and thought.

It is a place where artists, writers and researchers gather to
nourish public reflection about the issues of our time. Many
of our activities are devoted to international literature.

Among our recent guests: Russell Banks, Philippe Bourgois,
Charles Larmore, Dennis Cooper, Robert Coover, Don DeLillo,
David Flusfeder, Richard Ford, Philip Gourevitch,
Aleksandar Hemon, Benjamin Kunkel, Dennis Lehane,
Colum McCann, David Means, Toni Morrison,
Rick Moody, Jim Nisbet, Colson Whitehead,
John Edgar Wideman . . .

Translators in residence:

PEN American Center, the Cultural Services of the French
Embassies in New York and London, and the Villa Gillet
organise a series of translation residences during which
works of literature and social sciences written in the
French language are translated. Every year the Villa Gillet
welcomes 3 American and 3 British translators.
During these residencies, the Villa Gillet organises public
discussion forums with the translators on their current
projects as well as translation workshops.

International Forum on the Novel:

The Villa Gillet and *Le Monde des Livres* will organise, for the first time, the International Forum on the Novel in Lyon, from the 30th May to the 3rd June 2007.

This event will bring together 50 writers, literary journalists from Le Monde des Livres and literary critics of all nationalities. Amongst others, American authors Donald Antrim, Russell Banks, Nik Cohn, Charles D'Ambrosio, Colum McCann, Rick Moody . . . will be present.

Visit our website : www.villagillet.net

GRAND**LYON**
communauté urbaine

With 1.2 million inhabitants and 57 different communes, Lyon and its neighbouring suburbs, called the Urban Community of Lyon, know how to celebrate diversity. In the words of Charles Baudelaire, they try to bring together "the transient, the fleeting, the contingent" that is modernity with the other half of art, "the eternal and the immovable."

The city is set in magnificent surroundings—where Northern Europe meets the South and the rivers Saone and Rhone unite. Since ancient Roman times, it has grown gracefully, forging links with the outside and nurturing its thirst for culture and innovation.

It has come to be a place that embraces new ways of thinking, of building, of living and sharing life in the city. Where architecture is free to be different, with a more human dimension, and where nature plays a key role. A city bursting with energy, united and exciting, whose greatest ambition is to bring pleasure, desire, and the will to move forward together.

The Villa Gillet is one of the most successful examples of the boundless, artistic expression and creativity borne of this ambition.

The Urban Community of Lyon is pleased to celebrate its 20th anniversary by publishing this collection of short fictions which we hope will convey the diversity of talent that makes up the world we live in.

PETROS ABATZOGLOU, *What Does Mrs. Freeman Want?*
PIERRE ALBERT-BIROT, *Grabinoulor.*
YUZ ALESHKOVSKY, *Kangaroo.*
FELIPE ALFAU, *Chromos.*
  Locos.
IVAN ÂNGELO, *The Celebration.*
  The Tower of Glass.
DAVID ANTIN, *Talking.*
DJUNA BARNES, *Ladies Almanack.*
  Ryder.
JOHN BARTH, *LETTERS.*
  Sabbatical.
DONALD BARTHELME, *The King.*
  Paradise.
SVETISLAV BASARA, *Chinese Letter.*
MARK BINELLI, *Sacco and Vanzetti Must Die!*
ANDREI BITOV, *Pushkin House.*
LOUIS PAUL BOON, *Chapel Road.*
  Summer in Termuren.
ROGER BOYLAN, *Killoyle.*
IGNÁCIO DE LOYOLA BRANDÃO, *Teeth under the Sun.*
  Zero.
CHRISTINE BROOKE-ROSE, *Amalgamemnon.*
BRIGID BROPHY, *In Transit.*
MEREDITH BROSNAN, *Mr. Dynamite.*
GERALD L. BRUNS,
  Modern Poetry and the Idea of Language.
GABRIELLE BURTON, *Heartbreak Hotel.*
MICHEL BUTOR, *Degrees.*
  Mobile.
  Portrait of the Artist as a Young Ape.
G. CABRERA INFANTE, *Infante's Inferno.*
  Three Trapped Tigers.
JULIETA CAMPOS, *The Fear of Losing Eurydice.*
ANNE CARSON, *Eros the Bittersweet.*
CAMILO JOSÉ CELA, *The Family of Pascual Duarte.*
  The Hive.
  Christ versus Arizona.
LOUIS-FERDINAND CÉLINE, *Castle to Castle.*
  Conversations with Professor Y.
  London Bridge.
  North.
  Rigadoon.
HUGO CHARTERIS, *The Tide Is Right.*
JEROME CHARYN, *The Tar Baby.*
MARC CHOLODENKO, *Mordechai Schamz.*
EMILY HOLMES COLEMAN, *The Shutter of Snow.*
ROBERT COOVER, *A Night at the Movies.*
STANLEY CRAWFORD, *Some Instructions to My Wife.*
ROBERT CREELEY, *Collected Prose.*
RENÉ CREVEL, *Putting My Foot in It.*
RALPH CUSACK, *Cadenza.*
SUSAN DAITCH, *L.C.*
  Storytown.
NIGEL DENNIS, *Cards of Identity.*
PETER DIMOCK,
  A Short Rhetoric for Leaving the Family.
ARIEL DORFMAN, *Konfidenz.*
COLEMAN DOWELL, *The Houses of Children.*
  Island People.
  Too Much Flesh and Jabez.
RIKKI DUCORNET, *The Complete Butcher's Tales.*
  The Fountains of Neptune.
  The Jade Cabinet.
  Phosphor in Dreamland.
  The Stain.
  The Word "Desire."
WILLIAM EASTLAKE, *The Bamboo Bed.*
  Castle Keep.
  Lyric of the Circle Heart.
JEAN ECHENOZ, *Chopin's Move.*
STANLEY ELKIN, *A Bad Man.*
  Boswell: A Modern Comedy.
  Criers and Kibitzers, Kibitzers and Criers.
  The Dick Gibson Show.
  The Franchiser.
  George Mills.
  The Living End.
  The MacGuffin.
  The Magic Kingdom.
  Mrs. Ted Bliss.
  The Rabbi of Lud.
  Van Gogh's Room at Arles.

ANNIE ERNAUX, *Cleaned Out.*
LAUREN FAIRBANKS, *Muzzle Thyself.*
  Sister Carrie.
LESLIE A. FIEDLER,
  Love and Death in the American Novel.
GUSTAVE FLAUBERT, *Bouvard and Pécuchet.*
FORD MADOX FORD, *The March of Literature.*
JON FOSSE, *Melancholy.*
MAX FRISCH, *I'm Not Stiller.*
  Man in the Holocene.
CARLOS FUENTES, *Christopher Unborn.*
  Distant Relations.
  Terra Nostra.
  Where the Air Is Clear.
JANICE GALLOWAY, *Foreign Parts.*
  The Trick Is to Keep Breathing.
WILLIAM H. GASS, *The Tunnel.*
  Willie Masters' Lonesome Wife.
ETIENNE GILSON, *The Arts of the Beautiful.*
  Forms and Substances in the Arts.
C. S. GISCOMBE, *Giscome Road.*
  Here.
DOUGLAS GLOVER, *Bad News of the Heart.*
  The Enamoured Knight.
KAREN ELIZABETH GORDON, *The Red Shoes.*
GEORGI GOSPODINOV, *Natural Novel.*
JUAN GOYTISOLO, *Marks of Identity.*
PATRICK GRAINVILLE, *The Cave of Heaven.*
HENRY GREEN, *Blindness.*
  Concluding.
  Doting.
  Nothing.
JIŘÍ GRUŠA, *The Questionnaire.*
JOHN HAWKES, *Whistlejacket.*
AIDAN HIGGINS, *A Bestiary.*
  Bornholm Night-Ferry.
  Flotsam and Jetsam.
  Langrishe, Go Down.
  Scenes from a Receding Past.
  Windy Arbours.
ALDOUS HUXLEY, *Antic Hay.*
  Crome Yellow.
  Point Counter Point.
  Those Barren Leaves.
  Time Must Have a Stop.
MIKHAIL IOSSEL AND JEFF PARKER, EDS., *Amerika:*
  Contemporary Russians View
  the United States.
GERT JONKE, *Geometric Regional Novel.*
JACQUES JOUET, *Mountain R.*
HUGH KENNER, *The Counterfeiters.*
  Flaubert, Joyce and Beckett:
  The Stoic Comedians.
  Joyce's Voices.
DANILO KIŠ, *Garden, Ashes.*
  A Tomb for Boris Davidovich.
ANITA KONKKA, *A Fool's Paradise.*
GEORGE KONRÁD, *The City Builder.*
TADEUSZ KONWICKI, *A Minor Apocalypse.*
  The Polish Complex.
MENIS KOUMANDAREAS, *Koula.*
ELAINE KRAF, *The Princess of 72nd Street.*
JIM KRUSOE, *Iceland.*
EWA KURYLUK, *Century 21.*
VIOLETTE LEDUC, *La Bâtarde.*
DEBORAH LEVY, *Billy and Girl.*
  Pillow Talk in Europe and Other Places.
JOSÉ LEZAMA LIMA, *Paradiso.*
ROSA LIKSOM, *Dark Paradise.*
OSMAN LINS, *Avalovara.*
  The Queen of the Prisons of Greece.
ALF MAC LOCHLAINN, *The Corpus in the Library.*
  Out of Focus.
RON LOEWINSOHN, *Magnetic Field(s).*
D. KEITH MANO, *Take Five.*
BEN MARCUS, *The Age of Wire and String.*
WALLACE MARKFIELD, *Teitlebaum's Window.*
  To an Early Grave.
DAVID MARKSON, *Reader's Block.*
  Springer's Progress.
  Wittgenstein's Mistress.
CAROLE MASO, *AVA.*